Going Places

Written by Peter H. Reynolds and Paul A. Reynolds

Illustrated by Peter H. Reynolds

SCHOLASTIC INC.

Rafael had been waiting
all year long for the
Going Places contest,
a chance to build a go-cart,
race it . . . and win.

When their Teacher announced,
"Who would like the first kit?"
Rafael's hand shot up.

The rest of the class watched enviously as Rafael walked back to his seat with a kit.

Mrs. Chanda assured them, "Don't worry—you'll all be getting one . . .

. . . and they're all EXACTLY alike."

Grace

Billy

Jeannie

Leroy

Beyoncé

Violet

Kathy

Fiana

Elena

Holly

Raj

Henry

The kit came with a set of precise instructions. That made Rafael happy. He was very good at following directions.

Rafael hammered, glued, nailed, and assembled his kit.

His go-cart looked just like the one in the directions.
He was feeling quite proud.

Rafael wondered
how his classmate Maya was doing.
She lived right next door.

He peered over the fence.
"Hey, Maya, you haven't even started?!"

Maya didn't respond. She was so intent on watching the bird in front of her, and quickly sketching it, that she didn't even notice Rafael.

Then she just put down her pencil
and stared at the bird dreamily.

Rafael shrugged—and let her be.

The next morning Rafael checked back in to see how Maya was doing.

"Wow, what is that?" he asked.

Maya grinned. "You like it?"

Rafael responded slowly, "Yeeeaah—extremely cool.
But, uh, Maya, there's just one little problem.
That's not a go-cart."

Maya smiled. "Who said it HAD to be a go-cart?"

Rafael was confused. The set of instructions inside the box were for a GO-CART. But then again, they didn't say it HAD to be a go-cart. He looked again at Maya's contraption. After a moment, he grinned.

"I get it. Hey, Maya, I really want to win this race. The instructions never said we couldn't team up either!"

And so they did, working late into the evening.

The next day everyone gathered for the big race.
Each go-cart was a perfect replica of the other.

Except one.

One of the kids laughed. "Looks like you had trouble with the **Going Places** instructions. You're going places all right—you're GOING to lose!"

Maya and Rafael didn't even have time to respond because the announcer's big, boomy voice called out,

A buzzer sounded.

"And they're off!"

While all the other go-carts disappeared in a cloud of dust, Maya just sat there in their motionless vehicle. Rafael shouted over the roar of engines and cheering crowds. "Maya! What are we waiting for?"

"No worries, Rafael!" Maya answered.
"Flaps down, throttle up!"

And now THEY took off—off into the air!

The other contestants
looked up in amazement.

Maya and Rafael hovered and then sped past them all.

Before long, Maya and Rafael coasted across the finish line to the cheers of the waiting crowd.

They kept rolling clear across the race grounds. Maya slammed the brakes, stopping just short of the lake at the edge of the school field.

Rafael noticed a startled frog leap from a lily pad and dive into the water. He raised his eyebrow and looked at Maya. She smiled.

"Rafael, are you thinking what I'm thinking . . . ?"

Rafael just nodded.

To all the great thinkers
who have gone above and beyond.

And especially to Dan LeClerc, our tenth-grade
social studies teacher, who dared us to have original ideas.
—Peter and Paul

ISBN 978-0-545-84888-6

Text copyright © 2014 by Peter H. Reynolds and Paul A. Reynolds.
Illustrations copyright © 2014 by Peter H. Reynolds. All rights reserved.
Published by Scholastic Inc., 557 Broadway, New York, NY 10012,
by arrangement with Atheneum Books for Young Readers, an imprint of
Simon & Schuster Children's Publishing Division. SCHOLASTIC and associated logos
are trademarks and/or registered trademarks of Scholastic Inc.

12 11 10 9 8 7 6 5 4 3 2 1   15 16 17 18 19 20/0

Printed in the U.S.A.   40

First Scholastic printing, January 2015

Design by Ann Bobco
The text for this book is set in Carrotflower.
The illustrations for this book are rendered digitally.